Pinocchio

Dorling Kindersley
LONDON, NEW YORK, SYDNEY, DELHI,
PARIS, MUNICH and JOHANNESBURG

Senior Art Editor Jane Thomas
Senior Editor Marie Greenwood
Managing Art Editor Jacquie Gulliver
Picture Research Jo Walton
US Editor Constance Robinson
DTP Designer Kim Browne
Production Joanne Rooke

Published in the United States by Dorling Kindersley Publishing, Inc.
375 Hudson Street New York, New York 10014

First American Edition, 1999
Paperback edition published in 2000
4 6 8 10 9 7 5 3

Dorling Kindersley registered offices:
80 Strand, London WC2R 0RL

ISBN 0-7894-6112-9
A catalog record is available from the Library of Congress

Acknowledgments
The publisher would like to thank the following for their kind permission to reproduce their photographs:

a = above; c = center; b = below/bottom; l = left; r = right; t = top.
AKG London 16, 44 above; **British Museum** 20; **Corbis-Bettmann** 46 below left /Adam Woolfitt 45 center right;
Il Dagherrotipo inside cover flap, 48 above left, 48 below right, 48; **E.T. Archive** 14 right, 46 above; **Mary Evans
Picture Library** 35, 44 below center, 44 below left; **Robert Harding Picture Library** 24 /Roy Rainford 48 above
right; Hulton Getty 12; **Billie Love Historical Collection** 46 above right; **Moviestore Collection**/© Disney
Enterprises Inc. 46 below right; 46 center left; **Rex Features** 47 above right; **Scala/Centro Didattico Nazionale**,
Firenze 48 below left; **Telegraph Colour Library**/S Benbow 45 above right.

The publisher would particularly like to thank the following people:
The Puppet Centre, London; Andy Crawford and Gary Ombler (photography); Chris Molan (additional illustration);
Claire Ricketts, Sarah Stanley, and Claire Watson (design assistance); Alastair Dougall, David Pickering, and Nicholas Turpin
(editorial assistance). Lisa Lanzarini and Jane Thomas for artwork borders.

Color reproduction by Bright Arts
Printed in China by L.Rex Printing Co., Ltd.

For our complete
catalog visit
www.dk.com

DORLING KINDERSLEY CLASSICS

Pinocchio

By CARLO COLLODI

Translated and adapted by Jane Fior

Illustrated by
Simon Bartram

A Dorling Kindersley Book

Contents

~A Piece of Wood~

ONCE UPON A TIME …
"There was a king!" you will say right away.
But no, children, you are wrong.

Once upon a time there was a piece of wood.

It turned up in the workshop of Master Antonio, the carpenter, but just as he was sharpening his tools to make it into a table leg, a little voice cried out: "Don't hit me!"

Master Antonio thought he must be dreaming so he paid no attention. Instead he picked up his axe and brought it down hard.

"Ow! That hurt!" cried the same little voice. Master Antonio felt frightened but he told himself not to be foolish and reached for his other tools. As he began to push the plane backward and forward over the wood to smooth the surface, the little voice began to giggle. "Stop it, you're tickling me!" it said.

This time Master Antonio fell to the ground as if struck by lightning. When he opened his eyes, he found himself sitting on the floor. At that very moment there was a knock on the door.

"Come in," said Master Antonio, still in a daze. In came an old man in a yellow wig. His name was Geppetto.

"What are you doing on the floor?" asked Geppetto.

"Teaching the ants how to read!" said Master Antonio. "What can I do for you, my old friend?"

"I have come to ask you a favor," said Geppetto. "I want to make myself a beautiful puppet that will be able to jump and dance and turn somersaults. Do you have some wood for me?"

Master Antonio went right over to his bench and gave Geppetto the piece of wood that had frightened him so much, but as he did so the wood slipped through his fingers and hit poor Geppetto on the shin.

"OUCH!" said Geppetto. "This is a fine way to begin!" and he picked up the wood and limped home.

The piece of wood hit Geppetto on the shin.

Geppetto lived in a small ground floor room. He was very poor and for furniture he had a sagging bed, an old kitchen chair, and a rickety table.

As soon as he arrived home, he sat down and took up his tools. "What name shall I give this puppet?" he wondered. "I know, I'll call it Pinocchio."

Italian puppets were often worked by strings, but Pinocchio is unlike any other puppet. He can talk and move, and needs no puppeteer to guide him.

Once he had settled on a name, he set to work. Carefully he began to carve the puppet's head, then its hair, its forehead, and its eyes. When he had finished the eyes, he was astonished to find that they could move and indeed were staring at him. Geppetto felt quite uncomfortable.

Now it was time to carve the puppet's nose. To Geppetto's surprise, the minute he stopped carving, the puppet's nose began to grow and grow. Soon it was enormously long.

Next came the mouth. Geppetto carved a sweet expression but immediately the puppet began to grin and make horrible faces.

"Stop that," said Geppetto. In reply, the puppet stuck out its tongue!

As soon as the arms were carved, the puppet grabbed Geppetto's yellow wig and put it on his own head.

"You little scoundrel! You are not even finished and already you are behaving badly toward your father."

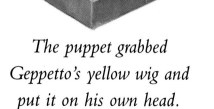

The puppet grabbed Geppetto's yellow wig and put it on his own head.

When Geppetto had carved the feet, Pinocchio took to his heels and ran out into the street. There he collided with a policeman who caught him by the nose and took him right back to Geppetto.

As soon as he saw the old man, Pinocchio threw himself to the ground and began to shout and wail. "Don't make me go back," he cried. "Please! Please!"

"Look at that poor little puppet," said a woman. "Geppetto may seem kind enough but who knows what he is really like? If the puppet is left here, perhaps Geppetto will break him in two."

A policeman caught Pinocchio by the nose.

When the policeman heard this, he arrested the protesting Geppetto and dragged him off to prison. Pinocchio, meanwhile, let himself into the house and with a sigh of relief bolted the door.

His satisfaction didn't last long.

Crick-crick-crick!

"Who is there?" cried Pinocchio, thoroughly frightened.

Cricket, "I've come to tell you something very important."

Pinocchio turned to see a large cricket climbing up the wall.

"What are you doing here?" said Pinocchio rudely.

"Listen," chirped the Cricket, "I've come to tell you something very important. Nothing good comes to children who disobey their parents and run away from home."

"Say what you like, Cricket, but I am leaving in the morning. I don't want to be sent to school like other children. I want to dance and sing and have fun."

"Foolish puppet," said the Cricket sadly. "I am sorry for you."

"Why do you feel sorry for me?"

"Because you're a puppet and because you've got a wooden head."

Pinocchio was so angry when he heard these words that he picked up a wooden mallet and hurled it. Perhaps he didn't mean to hurt him, but the mallet flattened the poor cricket and struck him dead.

The Talking Cricket tells Pinocchio how he should behave. But the puppet silences the Cricket's voice of good sense with a mallet.

Then Pinocchio realized that he was hungry. "That Talking Cricket was right," he thought. "If I hadn't run away, my father would be here to give me my supper. Now I will have to go and beg for something to eat."

It was dark outside. The wind was howling and the village street was empty. Pinocchio, his stomach rumbling, went up to a house and rang the bell.

An old man leaned out of the upstairs window. "What do you want at this hour of the night?" he shouted down.

"Please, a piece of bread," called Pinocchio.

The old man, thinking the puppet was up to mischief, fetched a

bucket of water and poured it over him.

Pinocchio dragged his way home, soaking wet and exhausted. He sat close to the stove to dry and soon dozed off. But, oh dear! While he was asleep his feet began to burn and soon turned to ashes.

At daybreak Pinocchio woke to hear Geppetto banging on the door, but he couldn't let him in because he had no feet.

The old man poured a bucket of water over the puppet.

Geppetto had to crawl in through the window. When he saw Pinocchio, he cried, "Oh my poor boy, what has happened to you?"

Sobbing loudly, Pinocchio told him the whole story.

Geppetto felt sorry for the puppet, but he said sternly, "Why should I make you new feet? You will only run away from home."

"Oh no, Papa, I promise I'll stay here with you and go to school and be good."

"Hmm," said Geppetto, but he fetched his tools and soon made two fine feet and stuck them neatly in place. "If you are to go to school, you will need some clothes," said Geppetto and he made Pinocchio a little suit of flowered paper, a pair of shoes, and a pointed hat. "I'll need a reading book too," said Pinocchio.

Geppetto looked worried. Then he put on his old coat and went out of the house. He returned in his shirtsleeves, a new reading book in his hand. "Where is your coat, Papa?" asked Pinocchio. When he realized that Geppetto had sold it to buy the book, Pinocchio threw his arms around his father and covered him with kisses.

Travelling puppet shows were popular in Europe. Harlequin and Punchinello were favorite Italian characters — Punch was based on Punchinello.

Now Pinocchio was ready to go to school. He said good-bye to Geppetto and set off down the street. In the square he met a crowd of people around a marquee. Over the entrance was a banner that announced:

GREAT PUPPET SHOW
Entrance five cents

"I want to go to that," said Pinocchio, forgetting his promises. "But how can I buy a ticket?"

"Sell me your book for five cents," said an old man standing beside him. Without a thought, Pinocchio parted with his book and made his way into the little theater.

The puppets saw Pinocchio and began to jump for joy.

The curtains parted and the play began. Harlequin and Punchinello came on stage, quarreling as they always did, and threatening to come to blows at any moment. Then the puppets saw Pinocchio sitting in the front row and they began to jump for joy. "Hey, Pinocchio!" they cried. "Come and join your wooden brothers." ✧

~ Five Gold Coins ~

A lame Fox and blind Cat came walking down the road.

PINOCCHIO HAD AN EXCITING TIME performing with the puppets and when it was time to leave, the Puppet Master presented him with five gold coins.

Pinocchio set off happily down the road but he had not gone far when he met a lame Fox and a blind Cat.

"Good morning, Pinocchio," said the Fox.

"Good morning, Pinocchio," repeated the Cat.

"How do you know my name?" asked Pinocchio, surprised.

"We know your father well," said the Fox. "Why, I saw him only yesterday, standing by his house, shivering in his shirtsleeves."

"He won't shiver much longer," said Pinocchio proudly, "for I have five gold coins and I am going to buy him a coat."

The Fox came closer. "Five coins aren't so many," he said. "Come with us to the Field of Miracles. If you bury your money tonight, when you go back in the morning, instead of five coins you will find two thousand!"

In many folk tales, foxes are portrayed as crafty characters who play tricks on others. This sly-looking fox is from an Aesop's fable.

What a wonderful plan! Pinocchio's new friends suggested they go to the inn first to eat and rest. They sat down to a lavish feast and then retired to their rooms. But at midnight, when it was time to leave, Pinocchio found that the Fox and the Cat had disappeared, leaving him to pay for their rooms and their supper. Now he only had four gold coins.

Pinocchio supposed his friends had gone on to the Field of

Miracles, and decided to follow them. On the way he saw a little creature sitting on a tree, glowing faintly. It was the ghost of the Talking Cricket! "Turn back, Pinocchio," he called. "Don't put your trust in those who promise to make you rich overnight."

"I am going to find the Fox and the Cat," said Pinocchio, "and make my fortune."

"Remember that children who always want their own way end up regretting it," said the Cricket, who then disappeared.

A cloud covered the moon. Suddenly, two dark figures covered in coal sacks jumped out of a ditch.

"Hand over your money," said one.

"Right away," said the other.

"No!" said Pinocchio, and off he ran.

"Turn back, Pinocchio," called the Talking Cricket.

Pinocchio could see a cottage in the distance. If only he could reach it! But it was no good – the two robbers caught up with him.

Pinocchio hid his four gold coins under his tongue, and although the angry robbers threatened him with all sorts of punishment, Pinocchio refused to spit them out.

Finally, the exasperated robbers tied him up and hung him from the branch of an oak tree. "We'll be back tomorrow," they said nastily. "By then you'll be ready to open your mouth."

Poor Pinocchio. He spent all night suspended from the tree, his arms and legs getting stiffer and stiffer. "Oh Papa," he cried. "If only you were here!"

It so happened that a beautiful Fairy with blue hair lived in the cottage. When she looked out of her window the next morning and saw the puppet dangling from the tree, she was filled with pity. The Fairy clapped her hands three times, one, two, three. Immediately a falcon flew through the air and landed on the window sill.

"I want you to peck the rope that binds that puppet with your strong beak," she commanded, "and put him gently on the ground."

The bird flew off and the good Fairy clapped her hands again. A splendidly dressed poodle appeared. He was the Fairy's coachman.

The Fairy's coach is like the fairy godmother's coach in Cinderella. *In that story, mice are turned into horses to pull the coach, and a rat becomes a coachman.*

"Medoro, harness my finest coach and take the road through the forest. At the foot of the Giant Oak you will find a poor puppet lying on the ground. Lift him up carefully, place him on the cushions in the coach, and bring him right back here to me."

As soon as the coach returned, pulled by a hundred pairs of white mice, the Fairy ran out. She took Pinocchio in her arms and gently carried him into the house. She put him to bed in a little bedroom, and sent for the most distinguished doctors in the district. Three arrived: a Raven, a Screech Owl, and a Talking Cricket.

"Tell me," said the Fairy, "is this puppet alive or dead?"

The Raven examined Pinocchio. "Certainly dead," he said.

"If he is not dead, he is certainly alive," said the Screech Owl.

The Cricket said, "I know this puppet. He is a scoundrel and a lazybones who has broken his father's heart."

When he heard these words, Pinocchio began to sob.

The beautiful Fairy carried Pinocchio in her arms.

Once the three doctors had gone, the Fairy put some powder into a glass and gave it to Pinocchio to drink.

"Is this medicine sweet or bitter?" said Pinocchio.

"It is bitter but it will do you good. Drink it up and I will give you a lump of sugar to take the taste away."

"I want my sugar lump **now**," demanded Pinocchio.

Pinocchio ate the sugar in an instant, but when the Fairy put the glass to his mouth, he pushed it away.

"I don't want that bitter medicine," he said.

"If you don't drink it, you won't get better," said the Fairy.

What a fuss Pinocchio made! He took the glass unwillingly, and sniffed at it. He put it to his lips. "It's too bitter," he said.

At last the Fairy persuaded Pinocchio to swallow it. Minutes later, Pinocchio jumped out of bed, feeling completely better.

"Come and tell me what has happened to you," said the Fairy, so Pinocchio sat on her lap and told her the whole story.

"Where are your gold coins now?" asked the Fairy.

"I've lost them," Pinocchio lied, for they were in his pocket. As he spoke, his nose grew six inches.

"Where did you lose them?"

"In the forest," said Pinocchio. At this

Pinocchio's nose was so long, he could not move.

second lie, his nose grew even longer.

"We can hunt for the coins then!" said the Fairy.

"Er, actually, I remember now, I didn't lose the coins. I swallowed them when I took your medicine."

Now his nose was so long he could not move. If he turned one way, he banged his nose on the bed. If he turned the other, he bumped it against the walls.

The Fairy began to laugh at him. "My dear Pinocchio," she said, "I do believe you are telling lies!"

Pinocchio felt so ashamed he did not know where to put himself. He tried to run out of the room, but his nose was so long, he could not go through the door!

The Fairy let Pinocchio cry and complain for half an hour before she took pity on him. Then she clapped her hands, and in flew a flock of woodpeckers, who pecked Pinocchio's nose down to size.

"How good you are to me, dear Fairy," said Pinocchio, drying his eyes. "I do love you."

Woodpeckers pecked Pinocchio's nose down to size.

"Then stay here with me," said the Fairy.

"What about my poor Papa?"

"He is on his way and will be here soon," said the Fairy.

"Really! Then I must go and meet him," cried Pinocchio, and he ran out of the house and down the path. But, oh dear, can you guess who he met as he went through the forest? The Fox and the Cat!

"Aha, there you are!" said the Fox. "We were looking for you. Come with us and bury your money."

Pinocchio met the Fox and the Cat once more.

Foolish Pinocchio! With dreams of riches, he followed the Fox and the Cat down the road.

They walked for half a day before they finally came to a bare field just outside a town.

"Here we are!" said the Fox. "Now you must dig a hole and bury your money. Cover it up, water it nicely, and then leave it for twenty minutes. When you come back, you will find that a little tree has already grown out of the soil, and its branches will be covered with gold coins."

Pinocchio did as he was told and, full of excitement, he thanked the Fox and the Cat a hundred times for their kindness.

"Don't mention it," said the Fox with a laugh.

"Don't mention it," repeated the Cat. Then the two said good-bye to Pinocchio and wished him a good harvest.

Pinocchio went for a walk and started counting the minutes. He kept thinking of all the delightful things he would buy with his money. He waited for a full hour, and then hurried back to the Field of Miracles, his heart beating as loudly as a grandfather clock. As Pinocchio drew near, he stopped and looked for the little tree, but he saw nothing. He went right over to the spot where he had buried his coins, but there was nothing growing there at all!

At that moment he heard someone screeching with laughter, and looking up he saw a large parrot grooming his feathers.

"What are you laughing at?" said Pinocchio angrily.

"I am laughing at a poor fool who believed everything he was told," said the parrot.

"What do you mean?" said Pinocchio.

"Ha-ha! While you were in the city, the Fox and the Cat came back and dug up your money. They pocketed it and took off like the wind."

Pinocchio began to cry. "How unhappy I am," he said. "I've lost my money and now I won't be able to buy my father a new coat. Why didn't I listen to everyone's advice? I'm going to go straight back to the Fairy's house to find my father and give him a big kiss. I'll tell him that from now on I will be a good boy and do what I am told." ✧

A fool and his money are soon parted. Having wasted one of his coins on Fox and Cat, Pinocchio has been tricked into leaving his other four coins where they can steal them.

"What are you laughing at?"
said Pinocchio to
the parrot.

～The Good Fairy ～

PINOCCHIO RAN ACROSS THE FIELD and did not stop for a second until he reached the road that led to the Fairy's house. As he rounded the bend on the hill, he looked down on the forest where he had first met the Fox and the Cat, but although he could see the Giant Oak rising up above the other trees, there was no sign of a roof or a chimney. Pinocchio had a sudden sad sort of feeling and he rushed toward the meadow where the little white house had once stood. It was no longer there. In its place was a marble slab – it was the Fairy's gravestone. You can imagine how dreadful Pinocchio felt when he read the sad words inscribed on it. He immediately broke into a terrible fit of weeping. He wept all night, and the following morning he was still sobbing.

HERE LIES THE FAIRY WITH BLUE HAIR WHO DIED OF GRIEF AFTER BEING ABANDONED BY PINOCCHIO

"Oh, dear Fairy, why did you die?" cried Pinocchio. "Tell me that it isn't true that you are dead. And where can my father be? Dear Fairy, I need to find him so that I can be with him, and never, ever leave him again. What will become of me now that I am alone in the world? Who will feed me? Where shall I sleep? Who will make me a new jacket? *Boo-hoo-hoo!*"

As Pinocchio lay sobbing on the ground, a large pigeon hovered above him on outstretched wings.

"What are you doing, child?" he called.

"Can't you see? I'm crying!" said Pinocchio, looking up and wiping his eyes on his sleeve.

"Tell me, do you happen to know a puppet called Pinocchio?"

"I'm Pinocchio," said the puppet, jumping to his feet.

"And do you know Geppetto too?" asked the bird.

"Do I know him? He is my father! Do you know where he is?"

"I left him three days ago on the seashore."

Pinocchio and the pigeon flew high in the sky.

"What was he doing there?"

"He was building a little boat to cross the ocean. He has been looking everywhere for you, and now he has decided to search in distant countries over the sea."

"Is it far to the seashore?" asked Pinocchio.

"More than a thousand miles," said the pigeon, "but if you climb on my back I will take you there."

Pinocchio climbed up, and soon they were flying so high they were nearly touching the clouds. Pinocchio grew curious and looked down, but the sight made him dizzy, so he held on tightly to the pigeon's neck. They flew and they flew, until at last they arrived at a beach. The pigeon set Pinocchio down next to a group of people who were waving and shouting and pointing out to sea.

"What is happening?" Pinocchio asked an old woman.

"There's a poor father out there who has lost his son and set sail to find him. But the sea is so rough, it looks as though the boat is about to capsize."

"That's my father!" shrieked Pinocchio. "I must rescue him!" And he dived into the stormy waves.

Since Pinocchio was made of wood, it was easy for him to float, and he could swim like a fish. He swam all night through rain, hail, thunder, and lightning, determined to reach his father's boat.

When morning came, he could see a long strip of land. It was an island in the middle of the sea. The tide was coming in, and the waves that tossed Pinocchio this way and that finally hurled him onto the pebbly beach.

Pinocchio saw a dolphin swimming close to the shore.

Pinocchio spread his clothes on the ground to dry and looked across the immense expanse of water for a sign of a boat, but all he could see was a large dolphin swimming close to the shore.

"Hello, may I have a word with you?" he called.

"Two if you like," replied the dolphin, who was very polite.

"Since you travel through sea by day and by night, have you by any chance seen a little boat with my father in it?"

"Who is your father?" asked the dolphin.

"The best man in all the world," declared Pinocchio.

"With last night's storm his boat will have sunk," said the dolphin. "And the shark who lives in these waters will have swallowed your father

Dolphins were known as kings of the sea, and thought to be helpful to humans. This kind, powerful creature is only too happy to help Pinocchio with his questions.

without a doubt."

Pinocchio's heart sank. What was he to do? He was frightened, and hungry too. Seeing a village in the distance, he set off for help.

It was Busy Bee Village and everyone was as busy as could be. When Pinocchio begged for some bread, no one would stop and listen until finally, a young woman took pity on him.

"Help me carry these jars of water home and I will feed you," she said.

As soon as they arrived at her house, she sat Pinocchio down at the table and made him a wonderful lunch. Gradually, Pinocchio's hunger eased, and he looked up from his plate at the kind young woman. No sooner had he looked at her face, than he let out a long Oooh! of surprise, and fell on his knees in front of her.

"What is the matter with you?" said the young woman, laughing.

"Oh, can it be? You have the same voice, the same eyes ... and the same blue hair! Oh Fairy, tell me that it is really you. I've cried and cried ever since I lost you."

And so saying, Pinocchio burst into tears, and flung himself into her arms.

"Oh Fairy, tell me that it is really you," cried Pinocchio.

The Fairy dried Pinocchio's tears. "I am surprised that you remember me," she said. "When you left, I was still young but now I am a grown woman, old enough to be your mother."

"I wish you *were* my mother," said Pinocchio sincerely. "And I wish I could grow too."

"Puppets don't grow, Pinocchio," said the Fairy.

"Then I don't want to be a puppet," said Pinocchio. "I want to be a real person."

"You could become real if you were good and went to school," said the Fairy.

"I was so sad when I read those words on the stone," said Pinocchio. "Tell me again that you're not really dead."

"I don't seem to be!" said the Fairy. "When I saw you crying, I forgave you. I knew then that you are good at heart and that is why I came here to look for you. I will be your mother if you will always obey me and do as I say."

Pinocchio learns his lessons well – but he still has much to learn about life. In his desire to be liked by everybody, he falls in with naughty schoolboys.

"I will, I will!" said Pinocchio, jumping for joy.

"Then you can begin by going to school tomorrow," said the Fairy.

They started to tease Pinocchio.

True to his word, the next day Pinocchio went to school. You can imagine how everybody laughed when they saw a puppet come into class. Worse, they started to tease him. One boy stole his hat, one pulled at his shirt, and another tried to draw moustaches under his nose. But in spite of this, Pinocchio did his best to be a good pupil. He arrived on time, paid attention in class, and did his homework. If he had one fault, it was that he wanted to be friends with everybody, and some of his classmates were naughty boys who didn't like school and fooled around.

This is why when one day a boy said, "We're going to the beach to see a shark. Do you want to come?" Pinocchio didn't stop to think. He tucked his school book under his arm and followed the boys down to the seashore. The sea was as calm as a mirror.

"Where is the shark?" asked Pinocchio.

"Perhaps he's having his breakfast," said one of the boys, snickering.

A full-scale fight broke out.

Pinocchio had been tricked, and worse was to come. One of the other boys punched him. Pinocchio hit back and in no time a full-scale fight had broken out. The shouts and screams brought two policemen to the scene and the boys all scattered. Only Pinocchio was left, and realizing he might be arrested, he began to run toward the beach.

The policemen set their big dog, a mastiff, after him. Panting, Pinocchio ran toward the sea and as soon as he was on the sand, he gave a great leap and dived into the water. The dog dived after him.

Unfortunately, Alidoro (that was the dog's name) could not swim and although he paddled hard to keep himself afloat, he soon began to go under.

"Help me! Help me!" barked the dog.

"Why should I?" said Pinocchio.

"Because if you don't, I will die," said the dog.

Pinocchio felt sorry for him. "Do you promise not to chase me?"

"I promise," said the dog. "Quick or I will drown."

"Help me! Help me!"
barked Alidoro.

Pinocchio hesitated for a moment, but Geppetto had told him that a good deed is never wasted so he swam toward Alidoro, seized his tail with both hands, and dragged him safely to shore. Then, still anxious about the policemen, Pinocchio jumped back into the water and began to swim toward a cave that he could see in the distance.

"Good-bye, Alidoro," he called.

"Good-bye, Pinocchio," replied the dog. "Thank you for saving my life. Remember, one good turn deserves another. I shall find a way to repay you."

As Pinocchio swam towards the cave, he was surprised to see a wisp of smoke rising above the rocks. "There must a be a fire in there," he said to himself. "Good, for I am very cold."

He had nearly reached the entrance when he felt something in the water lift him up and carry him through the air. He had been caught in a great net in which fish of every size and description were desperately wriggling and thrashing about.

At the same time he saw

By keeping his promise to Pinocchio, Alidoro, the mastiff police dog, teaches the puppet a lesson in loyalty.

a fisherman with a long white beard who was so old and so ugly that he looked like a sea monster. Pinocchio heard him say with glee, "What a catch! I shall have a fine meal tonight."

"It's a good thing I'm not a fish," said Pinocchio. But he spoke too soon. The fisherman put his hand into the net, pulled Pinocchio out, and tossed him

The fisherman was about to fry Pinocchio!

into a bowl of flour together with a handful of anchovies. Pulling himself up and peering over the rim, Pinocchio could see a large pan sizzling on the fire. Oh no! The fisherman was about to fry him and eat him for supper!

At that very moment a huge dog bounded into the cave, attracted by the smell of fish. It was Alidoro! "Save me, save me!" cried Pinocchio. Recognizing Pinocchio's voice, the dog snatched the floury puppet from the fisherman's hand. He rushed out of the cave and up the cliff path. As if he knew the way already, he ran all the way to the road and set Pinocchio gently on the ground. ✦

～ The Land of Toys ～

PINOCCHIO WENT to the Fairy's house and knocked on the door *rat-tat-tat*. He waited and waited and finally a snail appeared at the top window. "Who's that at this hour?" she called. "Pinocchio! I'm the puppet who lives here with the Fairy. Please hurry and open the door!"

"I'm coming," said the snail, "but, my boy, I'm a snail and snails never hurry."

Nine hours later, the front door finally opened and the helpful snail (who had done her very best) greeted Pinocchio, who was by now so weak with hunger that he fainted.

When he came to, he was lying on a sofa, with the Fairy bending over him. "Where have you been?" she said. "Why were you not at school?"

Feeling ashamed, Pinocchio confessed that he had run off with the other boys instead of staying and learning his lessons.

The Fairy looked

sad but she said she would forgive him one last time.

"I will be good," promised Pinocchio. "This time I really will."

"Then tomorrow your dearest wish will be granted," said the Fairy. "You will stop being a puppet and become a real boy. To celebrate, we will invite all your school friends to a party."

The Fairy set to work. She prepared two hundred cups of milky coffee and four hundred buttered buns.

Soon, everything was ready for the grand occasion. Pinocchio asked the Fairy if he could go and give out the invitations. He promised to be back before it was dark.

The Fairy kissed him good-bye. "Take care, Pinocchio," she said. "Promises are easy to make but they are easily broken too."

Pinocchio first went to find his friend Lampwick. He was one of the naughtiest boys in the school but Pinocchio was fond of him.

"I've come to invite you to my party," said Pinocchio, "for tomorrow I will become a real boy."

"I'm afraid I can't come," said Lampwick. "I'm leaving tonight – for the Land of Toys."

"The Land of Toys! What happens there?"

"Oh, it is a wonderful place," said Lampwick, "You just have fun from morning to night. There's no school! No books! No teachers! Why don't you come with me?"

"I promised the Fairy I would be home before dark," said Pinocchio, beginning to hesitate. "Are you going by yourself?"

"No, there will be a hundred of us. I am waiting for the coach."

The dusk was deepening, and in the distance they saw a tiny light moving along the road and heard the sound of bells jingling.

"There it is!" said Lampwick, jumping to his feet.

"*Is* it true that in that country boys never have to go to school?"

"Never," said Lampwick.

"Then I will come with you," said Pinocchio, his promises all forgotten.

"I'm coming," said the snail.

"All aboard for the Land of Toys!"

The coach, already full of boys, was a
splendid sight. It was drawn by twelve pairs of
little donkeys, all the same size and all wearing white
leather boots. The Coachman who had a face like a rosy
apple and a voice as smooth as butter called down, "All aboard for
the Land of Toys!"

Lampwick climbed up but Pinocchio suddenly thought of his
Fairy. "I'm going back home," he said.

*The donkey is a
symbol of stupidity.
Here, Pinocchio is
called a fool by a
donkey, before being
turned into a donkey
as a punishment for
his foolishness.*

"Don't leave. Come with us and have a
good time," shouted all the boys together.

Pinocchio sighed, and then he said,
"Move over. Make room for me."

"There's no room left," said the
Coachman. "If you want to come you'll
have to ride on one of my donkeys."

Pinocchio pulled himself onto the

donkey's back and the coach began to move off. As they galloped along the road, Pinocchio thought he heard a tiny voice saying, "You poor fool. You'll be sorry." And a little further on, he heard the same voice say, "Remember, stupid boy, that children who run away come to a bad end. One day you'll cry as I am crying now. But by then it will be too late."

Pinocchio shivered but he took no notice. He couldn't wait to get to the Land of Toys.

The coach arrived at daybreak and it was indeed a wonderful place. Children were playing everywhere – some were playing ball, some were turning somersaults, others were riding bicycles. One group was playing catch and another blind man's buff. Pinocchio and Lampwick joined in and made friends with everyone. Amid all sorts of pastimes, days and weeks flashed past.

After five wonderful months of playing about all day long, Pinocchio woke one morning to a horrible surprise. He put up his hand to scratch his head and found that he had grown – guess what? – donkey's ears!

"Oh no," shrieked Pinocchio. "What is happening to me?" He began to cry. "Oh why did I not listen to my Fairy? What am I to do?"

At that moment Lampwick arrived. Oh dear! Pinocchio saw that Lampwick too had long hairy ears. And that wasn't all. They found that they could no longer stand up straight but had to run around on all fours. And do you know what was the worst of all? When they opened their mouths to speak, all they could say was:

Hee-haw, Hee-haw!

There was a loud bang on the door. It was the Coachman. Before Pinocchio had time to lift the latch, the Coachman opened it himself by giving it a violent kick. "Well done, boys," he said, "you brayed very well. I recognized you immediately and here I am."

And he took out a currycomb and groomed the two donkeys till their coats shone like glass. Then he put halters on them and led them to market. For you see, the Coachman had a fine trade. Every now and then he would persuade all the naughty boys who hated school to jump in his coach. When it was full, he would drive to the Land of Toys. Here, the stupid boys would do nothing but amuse themselves until they turned into donkeys. Then the Coachman would drive them to market and sell them.

And so Lampwick was sold immediately to a peasant whose donkey had died the day before. Pinocchio was sold to a Ringmaster in a circus, who needed a donkey as part of his circus act.

Every day, the Ringmaster taught Pinocchio tricks. He had to learn how to jump through hoops, dance, and stand on his hind legs. If he made mistakes, the Ringmaster would whip him. It was a very hard life.

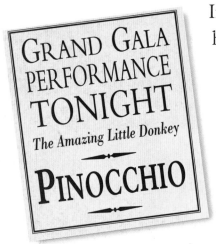

GRAND GALA PERFORMANCE TONIGHT
The Amazing Little Donkey
PINOCCHIO

At last the day came when Pinocchio was ready to appear in a special gala peformance with the other circus animals. All the seats were taken, full of boys and girls longing to see a donkey dance.

Soon the Ringmaster appeared and made an announcement: "Ladies and gentlemen! Please welcome a famous donkey who has already entertained all the Kings and Queens of Europe!" The audience cheered and Pinocchio trotted into the ring. Now the Ringmaster gave a deep bow and turning to Pinocchio, he said, "Before beginning your act, Pinocchio, bow to the ladies, gentlemen, and children." Pinocchio did as he was told.

"Now forward march!" Pinocchio had to walk, then trot, and

Performing animals were a top attraction at the circus. Sadly, they were often mistreated by their owners.

then gallop round the ring. As he galloped, the Ringmaster fired a pistol into the air and Pinocchio lay on the ground. It was then that he caught sight of a beautiful lady in the audience. She was wearing a gold chain around her neck from which hung a medallion. The picture on the medallion was of a puppet.

That is **my** picture, thought Pinocchio. That is **my fairy!** And he got up and went over to where she was sitting and cried, "Oh Fairy, dear Fairy!" But instead of these words, the sound that came out was a particularly loud **Hee-haw!**

The Ringmaster rushed over with his whip and beat the donkey on the nose, and when Pinocchio next looked at the audience, the Fairy had disappeared.

Pinocchio was now supposed to jump through a paper hoop, but he was crying so much that his back leg got caught and he fell to the ground. When the Ringmaster pulled him up, he could hardly walk. Poor Pinocchio was quite lame!

Pinocchio caught sight of a beautiful lady.

"That donkey's no use to me," said the Ringmaster. "Take him back to the market and sell him."

It didn't take long to find a buyer. A man who wanted to make a drum from the donkey's skin paid twenty cents for him. As soon as the deal was done, the man dragged poor Pinocchio down to the seashore. There he tied a stone around the donkey's neck and a long rope around one of his legs. Holding onto the rope, he knocked him into the water. Weighted down by the stone, Pinocchio quickly sank to the bottom of the sea. The man sat on the rock to wait.

After fifty minutes, he muttered to himself, "My donkey will be well and truly drowned by now." He began to pull on the rope. At last – guess what came to the surface – a live puppet, wriggling like an eel! The man thought he must be dreaming.

"Where is the little donkey I threw into the water?" he cried.

"The sea plays funny tricks sometimes!" said Pinocchio. "Do you want to know how it happened? Untie my leg and I will tell you." The man undid the rope and, free at last, Pinocchio sat down and told the man his story. He also told him all about the good Fairy.

"You see, she is my mother and like all good mothers, she looks after me. When she saw that I might drown, she sent a shoal of fishes along. They thought I really was a dead donkey and they began to eat me. By the time they had finished, all that was left was my hard wooden body and of course they couldn't eat that."

"That's all very well," said the man, annoyed, "but I gave twenty cents for you and I want my money back. I'll sell you for firewood."

"Sell me if you like," said Pinocchio. "I don't care!" And he jumped back into the water. "Good-bye, master," he called. "If you ever need a little bit of dry wood, remember me!"

Pinocchio swam quickly out to sea. After a while, he caught sight of a reef in the middle of the ocean. It was as white as marble and Pinocchio could see a goat standing on top of it. The goat's coat was a very odd color. Instead of being white or brown, it was a deep dark blue and it reminded Pinocchio of the Fairy's hair.

Pinocchio's heart began to thump and he swam as fast as he could toward the reef. But – oh dear! – when he was almost there, the horrible head of a sea monster reared up. It had an enormous mouth and three rows of teeth. Can you guess what it was? Yes, you are right. It was the terrible shark and he started to chase Pinocchio, his great jaws wide open, his sharp teeth poised.

Faster and faster swam Pinocchio. He had nearly managed to reach the reef when the shark caught up with him. Opening his jaws wide, he swallowed Pinocchio down in one gulp. ✧

The shark stretched his great jaws wide open.

～ Inside ～ the Shark

H OW DARK IT WAS inside the shark! Pinocchio tried to make out where he was but he could not see a thing. "Help! Help!" he cried tearfully. "Is there nobody here to rescue me?"

"There's no escape from here," said a voice in the darkness. It was a tuna fish that had been swallowed at the same time as Pinocchio. "All we can do is wait until we are digested."

"Digested! I don't want to be digested," said Pinocchio. "I want to get out of here."

"How do you expect to do that?" said the tuna fish. "The shark is more than a mile long, not counting his tail."

As they were talking, Pinocchio thought he could see a glimmer of light in the distance. "Look there," he said. "Perhaps that is an old fish who knows the way out. I am going to see."

"Good-bye and good luck," said the tuna fish.

Pinocchio began to grope his way along the inside of the shark, taking one step at a time toward the light. The further he went, the brighter and more distinct it became, and when at last he arrived, what do you think he found? You will never guess!

He found a little table laid for
supper, with a lighted candle stuck in a
green glass bottle. Sitting at the table was an old
man with a beard as white as snow. Pinocchio
opened his mouth in amazement. He rushed over and
flung his arms around the old man's neck.

"Papa! I have found you at last."

"Can it be?" said the old man, rubbing his eyes. "Can it
really be my dear Pinocchio?"

"Papa, I heard that your ship went down in the storm."

"Yes, my boat capsized in the sea. As I was floundering in the
water, the shark saw me and he put out his tongue and swallowed
me as easily as a piece of candy."

"How long have you been shut up in here?" asked Pinocchio.

"Two whole years," replied Geppetto. "Luckily, in the storm, a
merchant ship went down too. All the sailors were saved but the boat
went to the bottom of the sea and the shark, who was feeling
particularly hungry that day, swallowed it as well as me. I have
been living on the ship's provisions. But there is nothing more in
the pantry and this candle you see burning is the very last one."

"Papa, we must escape," said Pinocchio. "Follow me,
and do not be afraid."

*Sitting at the table was an old
man with a white beard.*

Pinocchio picked up the candle and, walking in front to light the way, he said to his father, "We must swim through the shark's mouth and throw ourselves into the sea."

"That's all very well, Pinocchio, but I can't swim."

"You can get on my back and I will carry you to shore. I am a good swimmer."

Geppetto shook his head sadly. "How can a little puppet be strong enough to carry me?"

"Wait and see," said Pinocchio. "Everything is going to be fine." They walked for some time through the shark's stomach, and eventually they reached the beginning of his throat. Luckily,

Pinocchio led the way with a lighted candle.

because the shark was very old he slept with his mouth open. When Pinocchio looked up the long expanse of throat he could see a patch of starry sky and brilliant moonlight.

"Now is the time to go," he whispered. "The shark is sleeping and the sea is calm. Follow me, Papa, and we shall soon be safe."

So up they climbed till they reached the monster's mouth. They

tiptoed carefully along his tongue and then, fearfully, crossed the three rows of teeth. Just as they were about to jump into the sea, the puppet said, "Climb on my back, Papa, and hold tight."

As soon as Geppetto was settled, Pinocchio jumped into the sea and began to swim for shore. It was a long way, and Pinocchio could feel his father shivering. "Take heart, Papa. In a few minutes we shall reach land," said Pinocchio to comfort him.

"But all I can see is sea and sky," said Geppetto, his teeth chattering. Pinocchio did his best to appear calm, but he was beginning to grow tired and the shore was still a long way off. "Oh, help me," he groaned. "Or we shall both die."

In the biblical tale, Jonah survives being swallowed by a whale, and is given another chance to be good, just as Pinocchio is.

"Here, take my tail," said a voice. It was the tuna fish. He had escaped through the shark's mouth at the same time as Pinocchio and Geppetto.

Gratefully, Pinocchio accepted his invitation but instead of holding onto his tail, they rode on his back.

In no time at all, they reached the shore. Pinocchio thanked the fish and kissed him affectionately, then offered Geppetto his arm.

Pinocchio and Geppetto rode on the fish's back.

"Lean on me, Papa," he said. "From now on, I am going to be a good boy and look after you."

Pinocchio and Geppetto had not gone very far when Pinocchio saw two familiar figures, the Fox and the Cat, begging at the side of the road. They were almost unrecognizable. The Cat had pretended to be blind for so long that finally he had become so, and the Fox, mangy and moth-eaten, had lost his tail.

"Oh Pinocchio," whined the Fox. " Have pity on us. Spare a penny for two poor cripples."

Pinocchio was not going to be tricked again. Instead he led Geppetto to a nearby house and knocked on the door. Can you guess who answered it? The Talking Cricket!

"Oh Cricket," said Pinocchio, remembering their last meeting and feeling ashamed. "Please forgive me and take pity on my father who needs a bed and something to eat."

The Cricket said he would and that they could stay with him if Pinocchio was prepared to work for his keep. Pinocchio agreed gladly. He soon learned how to make baskets out of reeds that he sold at market. In the evenings he taught himself to read and to write. Life was good for Geppetto and Pinocchio. Only

The Talking Cricket answered the door.

When Pinocchio becomes a real boy it means he has grown up. He is no longer the naughty child who thinks only of himself.

one thing troubled the puppet. What had happened to the good Fairy?

"Oh, haven't you heard?" said the Cricket. "She is seriously ill and too poor even to buy a crust of bread."

"I must help my poor Fairy," said Pinocchio. "I have four pennies saved. I shall take them to her tomorrow."

That night, when Pinocchio was asleep, he dreamed he saw the Fairy. She was smiling. She kissed him and said, "Dear Pinocchio, because of your kind heart, I forgive you all your past misdeeds. Boys who look after their parents in poverty and sickness deserve praise and love. Be good in the future, and you will be happy."

At this point the dream ended and Pinocchio woke up. He blinked and looked around him. Instead of a cottage bedroom, he was in an elegant room, and a smart new suit was laid ready for him by the side of the bed.

Pinocchio put it on and went to look at himself in the mirror. And what did he see? Instead of a puppet, there stood a boy with chestnut hair and blue eyes. A real boy! How could this be? Pinocchio ran to the next room.

"Papa, Papa, look at me!"

"My dear Pinocchio," said Geppetto, giving him a hug. "This is your gift from the Fairy. You see, when naughty boys mend their ways, they make everyone around them very happy."

"And what has happened to the old wooden Pinocchio?"

Gepetto pointed to a puppet sitting on a chair, his arms and legs dangling. He looked as though he could not possibly stand upright. "How funny I looked when I was a puppet!" said Pinocchio. "How good my Fairy is, for surely I am the happiest boy in the whole wide world." ✧

"Papa, look at me, I'm a real boy!"

Puppet Show

WHEN PINOCCHIO comes on stage to join his wooden friends, Harlequin and Punchinello, the theater is packed with people being entertained by puppets acting out fights, comedies, and love stories. Puppet shows were held throughout Europe at the time *Pinocchio* was written, more than 100 years ago.

Puppet theaters were especially popular in Italy, where Pinocchio *is set. The word puppet comes from the Italian* pupa, *meaning doll.*

✦ COMIC CHARACTERS
Punchinello and Harlequin were based on leading characters in Italian comic plays, known as the Commedia dell'Arte (comedy of art). In these plays, actors wore masks and mimed.

Harlequin (far left) and Punchinello

✦ PUPPET TYPES
The puppets in *Pinocchio* are marionettes – they are worked by strings. But there are many other kinds of puppets.

Glove puppets, like this version of Punchinello, are worn as gloves by the puppeteer, whose fingers make the puppet's head and arms move.

This ballet dancer is a marionette. The puppeteer pulls the strings to make her jump, dance, and skip — just like a real person.

✦ PUPPET PERFORMERS

From the late 1600s, the beak-nosed, cowardly Punchinello became known in Britain as Punch. He was soon joined by his wife, Judy (originally called Joan). Punch and Judy shows are still loved by British children, especially at the seaside.

Finger puppets are miniature glove puppets that fit over the finger of the puppeteer, who waggles his or her finger to make the puppet move.

This rod puppet is worked from below by rods. She can move more slowly and smoothly than a marionette.

The Story of a Puppet

PINOCCHIO – the rebel puppet with no strings – first came to life in Italy in the 1880s and was soon loved by children everywhere. *The Adventures of Pinocchio* is one of the most translated books in the world, and the puppet has gone on to star on the big screen.

Pinocchio is created, early 1900s

Pinocchio with Fox and Cat, 1914

© Disney

Pinocchio, *1940.*

✧ PUPPET STAR
In 1940 Walt Disney produced an enchanting animated version of *Pinocchio* which included the classic songs, "When You Wish Upon a Star" and "I've Got No Strings." The story was changed – the Fairy breathes life into the puppet, and the Cricket is called Jiminy – but the main idea remained the same.

✧ NOSE TROUBLE
Pinocchio's nose is legendary. When the puppet tells lies to the Fairy, his nose grows to ridiculous lengths. In Italy, there are several popular sayings that link noses with deceit, such as, "Your lie is running up your nose," meaning the lie is obvious to everyone!

✧ PINOCCHIO'S QUEST

The story of Pinocchio is like a journey through life. The puppet meets a variety of characters, good and bad, along the way, and has to decide how to behave. Time and again, Pinocchio is influenced into doing wrong. But eventually, the puppet learns loyalty toward the Fairy and Geppetto. At this point, he becomes a boy – he has learned how a real human should behave.

Scene from the 1997 film of Pinocchio

✧ FOX AND CAT

Pinocchio soon falls in with the devious Fox and Cat. These darkly comic characters find it easy to persuade the innocent Pinocchio to give away his money.

✧ CRICKET

The wayward Pinocchio fails to listen to the wise words of the Talking Cricket, until they are reunited at the end of the story.

BAD   **GOOD**

✧ LAMPWICK

Naughty schoolboy Lampwick tempts Pinocchio away from his studies to the idle, free and easy life of the Land of Toys. After this comes Pinocchio's most degrading moment, when he turns into a donkey.

✧ BLUE FAIRY

The Fairy guides and protects Pinocchio like a mother does her child. She is a mysterious figure – appearing and reappearing in different forms – and her blue hair adds to her mystery and magic.

Collodi's Story

*Carlo Collodi
1826–1890*

Carlo Lorenzini (Collodi) was born in Florence, Italy. As a child, he spent many happy years at school

Florence, Collodi's birthplace

in his mother's home village, fooling around with other boys – just like Pinocchio does. The village was called Collodi, the name Carlo later adopted as a pen name.

An Italian village school in the 1800s.

✧ EDUCATION FOR ALL

Collodi became a journalist and began to write plays and novels. Italy was then made up of many states, and Collodi joined the fight to make Italy a unified democracy. Collodi believed every child should have an education. This is reflected in *Pinocchio* where the puppet is encouraged to go to school.

✧ PINOCCHIO COMES TO LIFE

In 1881, Collodi wrote a serial called "The Story of a Puppet" for a children's newspaper. It ended with the puppet being hanged from a tree, but the story was so popular that Collodi wrote another version with a new title, *The Adventures of Pinocchio*. The book soon followed in 1883.

Pinocchio with the Fox and Cat, from the first edition of Pinocchio *illustrated by Enrico Mazzanti.*